D1275599

GRANDMA'S HANDS

written and illustrated by Dolores Johnson

MARSHALL CAVENDISH   NEW YORK

Marshall Cavendish Corporation, 99 White Plains Road, Tarrytown, New York 10591
The text of this book is set in 16 point Berkeley Medium
The illustrations are rendered in watercolor on paper
Printed in Italy
1 2 3 4 5 6 First edition

Library of Congress Cataloging-in-Publication Data
Johnson, Dolores.
Grandma's hands / illustrated and written by Dolores Johnson.   p.   cm.
Summary: While staying on his grandmother's farm, an African-American boy
learns that every child needs a home where there's love,
even though that love may be rough and scratchy.
ISBN 0-7614-5025-4
[1. Grandmothers—Fiction. 2. Love—Fiction. 3. Afro-Americans—Fiction.]
I. Title. PZ7.J631635Gr 1998 [E]—dc21 97-6129 CIP AC

To Hazel Ridgeway,
in celebration of the
23 years she devoted
to children at the
Inglewood Public
Library.

My mother told me it was time I got out of the city and she brought me to my grandmother's farm. She said, "I'm placing you in your grandma's hands." (I looked at those hands. They were wrinkled and veined and they were not as soft as my mother's.)

"I need to get myself together," my mother said. (I looked at her. She *did* seem to be coming apart.) "I'll write. Will you write me?" And before I had a chance to say "I wouldn't have to write if I could stay with you!" she left. I had to blink really hard to keep from blubbering.

My grandma told me,
"You better let it out, boy, or
you're goin' to blow up like
one of those big balloons in
that Thanksgiving parade
and float away. How's an
old lady like me goin' to
pull you out of the trees?"
So I laughed instead of cried,
and by the time I looked
around, I almost forgot I had
been left behind.

My grandma drove me from the train station in a wagon behind a big old brown horse that looked like it could barely stand, never mind walk. "I'm goin' to teach you how to ride old Nellie. I'm training her to race in the Kentucky Derby."

"You think I can ride a horse in the Kentucky Derby?"
I asked my grandmother, my heart pounding. This might
not be so bad after all.

"No, I'm goin' to teach you how to train her. *I'm* goin'
to be the jockey," she said as she coaxed the horse to go
a half step faster. And I stole a glance to see if she was
smiling. But I saw that a smile would feel like a stranger
on *that* face.

When I got to her farm, my grandmother showed me my bedroom. It was a little square place with just a quilt-covered bed and a handmade table and dresser. Then she showed me the barn she told me I was expected to shovel and sweep. She showed me the pen with the pigs she said that it was my job to feed. Then she said, "Stop squinching your face up like that, or you'll scare my chickens so bad they'll be laying scrambled eggs tomorrow."

My grandma probably knew all there was to know about scaring things. Her face was a mask of wrinkles. She looked older than the red dirt that filled the air and covered my socks and sneakers. Grandma was my mom's mother, and had the same creases between her eyes like my mom did. I hadn't really seen my grandmother in a long, long time.

That was back when I was a little kid, and my father was still with us. Now I only get a phone call from him on my birthdays. And I've only received two single-page letters from my mom in the week I've been here.

Dear Billy, Still looking for a job, the first letter said.

Got a job, but it wasn't right for me, the second letter said. And they both ended with, *Miss you. Stay strong. Your Mom.*

That night I lay in my bed holding the letters close to my face so I could still smell their perfume. I was thinking about how it seemed I never was going to get a chance to see her again, or play baseball with my friends. I was stuck in a place where there were no housing projects surrounded by fences and green-painted asphalt like in normal neighborhoods. And worst of all, I had to live with an old woman who must not have known anything about raising kids, cause she didn't seem to do a very good job with my mom.

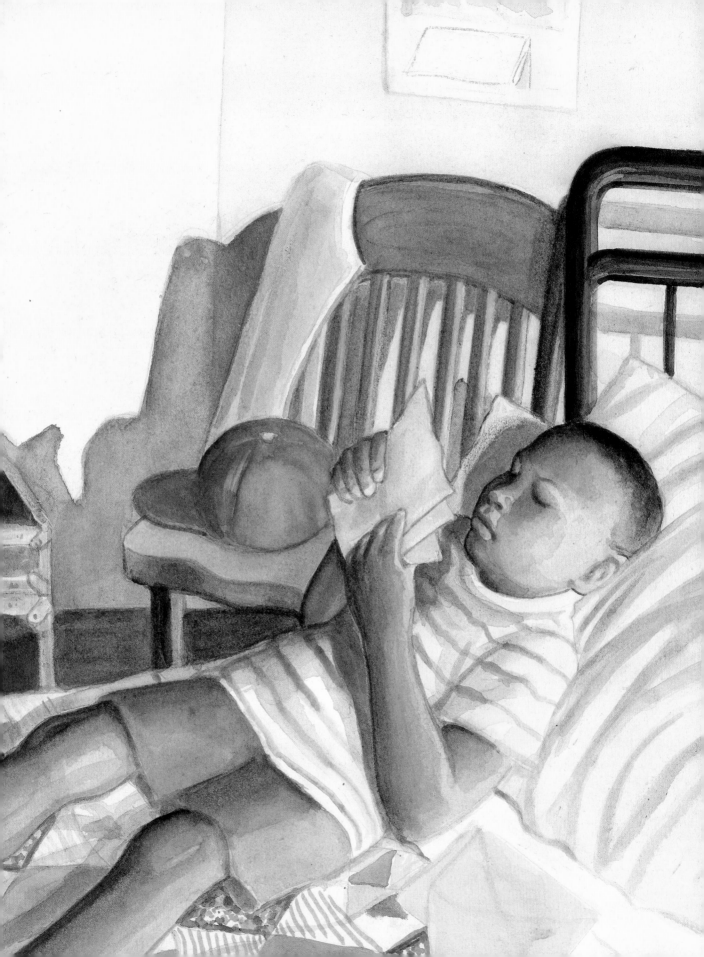

But before I fell asleep, my grandma brought in a glass of milk and a plate with some cookies. "These are star cookies that can only be found in the country," she told me. "They are made out of the same stuff as the stars in the skies. If you eat one before you fall asleep, as soon as you dream, you can climb on a star and take it wherever you want to go." That night I traveled to a place where my mother, father and I were all together again.

I spent the summer helping to tend the crops in the garden beside my grandma. I had never seen a sky so blue, nor smelt the earthy smell of worms before. I spent most of my time on my knees pulling carrots, radishes and potatoes out of the moist ground. "Grandma. Help! There must be a kid pulling at my roots from the other side of the world." Both of us pulled and tugged until we fell down laughing in the dirt.

I did my chores every day, and in time, I had to do my homework. The whole summer had passed, and my mother had not come to get me. School started, and every afternoon, as soon as I got off the school bus, I looked to see if she had sent me letter number three. After all, I had sent her at least twenty-five, twenty-six letters in the first week alone, asking her to bring me home.

After supper, Grandma often stood out with me in the cow pasture, and after a while she learned to throw a decent curveball. I must have swung my bat at that ball at least a thousand times. When I finally hit the ball hard enough so that it sailed over her head, she said, "Boy, I knew you could do it!" When I spent too long celebrating she said, "That ball won't get up off the ground and walk back over to us. Now go on and get it."

My grandmother didn't seem to
be gray-haired or old the day I ran
to tell her Kitty had just had her
babies. She just scampered up
that ladder in the barn, like she
was even younger than I. But
when she got to the top and saw
that Kitty was all right she leaned
up against the wall just panting.

"Whew! If I had to climb one
more step, the next thing I'd be
doing is trying on new angel
wings in heaven."

After we counted Kitty's seven
babies, Grandma told me, "You
can be the one to name them . . . "
that is, until I wanted to name
one of them Mama's name.
And then, in a huff she said,
"Don't bother to give them
any more names. They're
only going to be
given away."

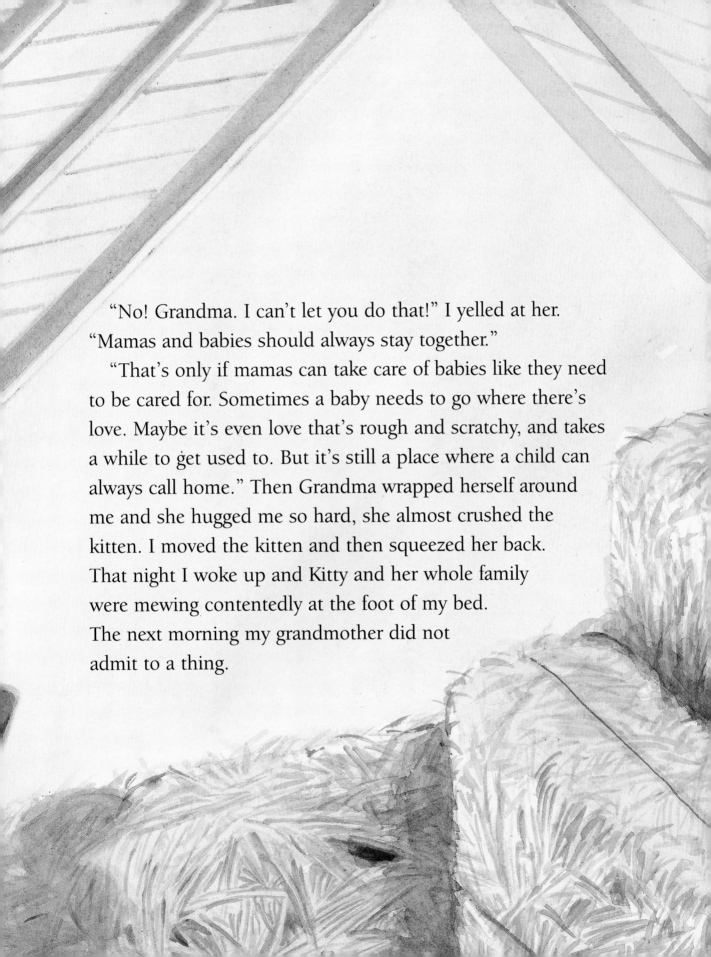

"No! Grandma. I can't let you do that!" I yelled at her. "Mamas and babies should always stay together."

"That's only if mamas can take care of babies like they need to be cared for. Sometimes a baby needs to go where there's love. Maybe it's even love that's rough and scratchy, and takes a while to get used to. But it's still a place where a child can always call home." Then Grandma wrapped herself around me and she hugged me so hard, she almost crushed the kitten. I moved the kitten and then squeezed her back. That night I woke up and Kitty and her whole family were mewing contentedly at the foot of my bed. The next morning my grandmother did not admit to a thing.

It was spring and the flowers were blooming in Grandma's garden when I next saw my mom. She didn't say hello when she appeared at the door, or even give me any excuses. She just said, "Now it's time for you to come home."

"But I am home," I told her again and again.

She asked, "What about your letters?"

I told her, "I don't mean them anymore."

She said, "It doesn't really matter. I need you with me." She climbed the stairs up to my room and packed my suitcase without any help from me.

I didn't blubber when I climbed into my mother's new car, even when I saw the tears that filled my grandma's eyes. Nor did I cry when I felt Grandma's rough hands softly stroking my cheek. But I had to let it all out after we drove out of her sight and I found a napkin filled with the smell of something wonderful on the seat beside me.

Though I did get a chance to live with my grandma two more summers, I still miss her. Yet, whenever I smell something sweet, see stars, or dream dreams, I am back in my grandma's hands.